E   Hurwitz, Johanna.
HUR   Ethan at home.

$12.99

30061000027314

HELPING YO

Here's how to make first-
reading easy and fun:

▶ Read the introduction at the
beginning of each story aloud.
through the pictures together s
your child can see what happe
story before reading the words

▶ Read the first page to your c
placing your finger under each

▶ Let your child touch the word
read the rest of the story. Give
her time to figure out each new

▶ If your child gets stuck on a wo
you might say, "Try something. L
the picture. What would make s

DATE
NOV 0 2 2012 MAY 0 3 2010 DEC 1 9 2012
NOV 18 '04 OCT 2 1 2005 JUN 6 2007
DEC 2 0 04 DEC 2 9 05 DEC 07 2005
10.5 NYC DEC 1 9 2005 NOV 0 5 2010
JAN 2 8 '05 MAR 2 5 2016
JUN 9 '05 SEP 2 5 2006 DEC 0 4 2009
DEC 1 5 2006 JAN 2 7 2011

Library of Congress Cataloging-in-Publication Data

Hurwitz, Johanna.
Ethan at home / Johanna Hurwitz ;
illustrated by Brian Floca. —1st ed.
p.   cm.   (Brand new readers)
Summary: Four simple stories about a young boy at bedtime,
when he is sick, getting ready to play in the snow, and
helping his mother clean the house.
ISBN 0-7636-1093-3
[1]. Bedtime—Fiction. 2. Sick—Fiction.
3. Snow—Fiction. 4. Cleanliness—Fiction.]
I. Floca, Brian, ill. II. Title. III. Series.
PZ7.H9574 Es 2003
[E]—dc21   00-037965

2 4 6 8 10 9 7 5 3 1

Printed in China

This book was typeset in Letraset Arta.
The illustrations were done in
watercolor and ink.

Candlewick Press
2067 Massachusetts Avenue
Cambridge, Massachusetts 02140

visit us at www.candlewick.com

ETHAN AT HOME

Johanna Hurwitz   ILLUSTRATED BY **Brian Floca**

CANDLEWICK PRESS
CAMBRIDGE, MASSACHUSETTS

Contents

ETHAN AND THE SNOW

Introduction

This story is called *Ethan and the Snow*.
It's about what happens when Ethan sees snow.
He puts on his scarf, coat, and hat. When
Ethan is ready to go out, he can't move.

Ethan sees snow.

Ethan puts on his scarf.

Ethan sees more snow.

Ethan puts on his coat.

Ethan sees MORE snow.

Ethan puts on his hat.

Ethan is ready to go out.

But Ethan can't move.

ETHAN SNEEZES

Introduction

This story is called *Ethan Sneezes*. It's about how Mom tries to help Ethan stop sneezing. She gives him juice, soup, and a blanket. When Ethan stops sneezing, Mom sneezes!

Ethan sneezes.

Mom gives him orange juice.

Ethan sneezes.

Mom gives him hot soup.

Ethan sneezes.

Mom gives him a blanket.

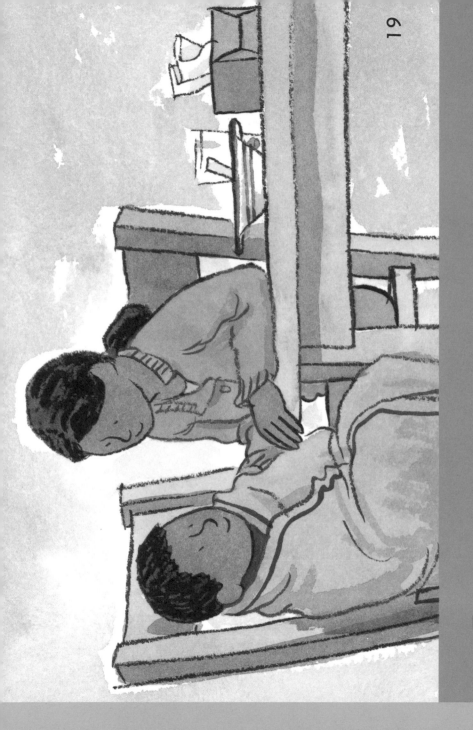

Ethan stops sneezing.

Mom sneezes.

ACHOO!

ETHAN CLEANS

Introduction

This story is called *Ethan Cleans*.
It's about how Ethan helps Mom clean.
Ethan sweeps, mops, washes, and dusts.
When the room is clean, Ethan is messy.

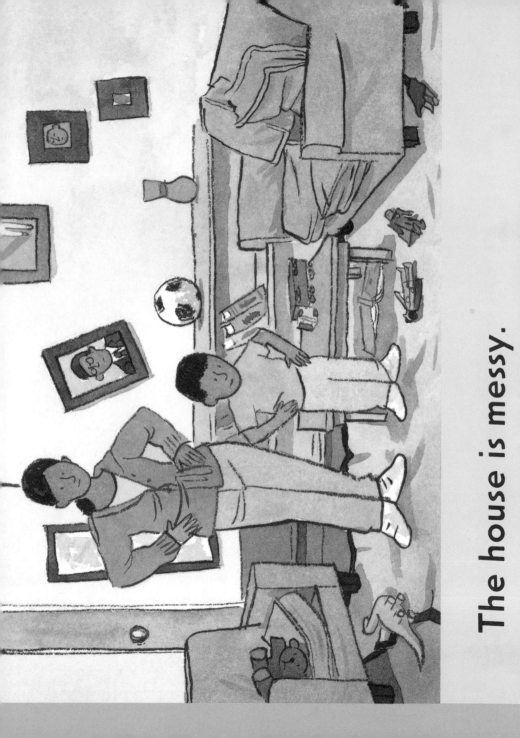

The house is messy.

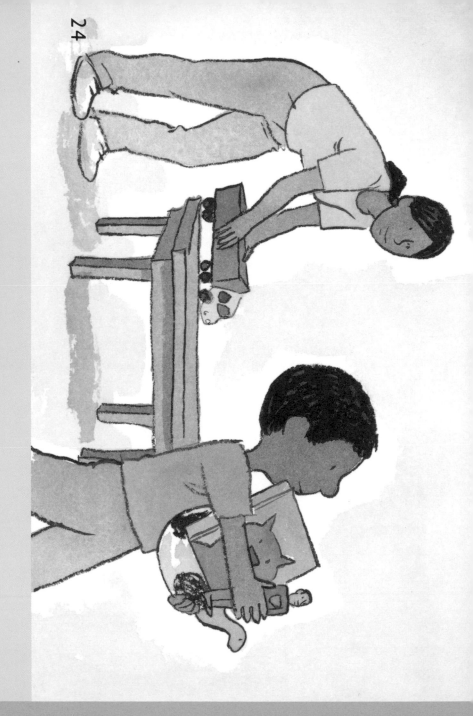

Ethan helps Mom clean.

Ethan sweeps.

Ethan mops.

Ethan washes.

Ethan dusts.

Now the house is clean.

But Ethan is messy.

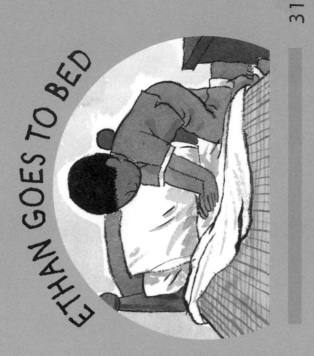

ETHAN GOES TO BED

Introduction

This story is called *Ethan Goes to Bed*. It's about how Ethan gets his bears, trucks, books, ball, and dinosaurs. When Ethan puts everything in his bed, he can't sleep.

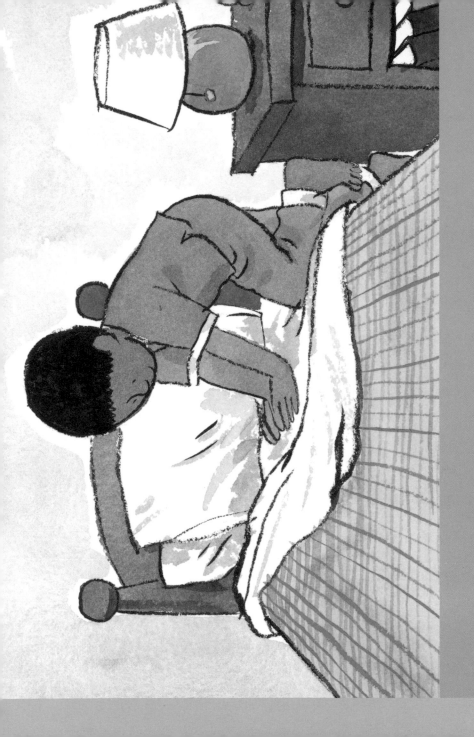

Ethan is going to bed.

Ethan gets his bears.

Ethan gets his trucks.

Ethan gets his books.

Ethan gets his ball.

Ethan gets his dinosaurs.

Ethan turns off his light.

But Ethan can't sleep.